#3

TEAM PLAYER

#3
TEAM PLAYER

Dean Hughes

Aladdin Paperbacks

First Aladdin Paperbacks edition, April 1999

Copyright © 1999 by Dean Hughes

Aladdin Paperbacks
An imprint of Simon & Schuster
Children's Publishing Division
1230 Avenue of the Americas
New York, NY 10020

Also available in an Atheneum Books for Young Readers edition.

Designed by Amanda Foley

The text of this book was set in Caslon 540 Roman

Printed and bound in the United States of America

10   9   8   7   6   5   4   3   2   1

The Library of Congress has cataloged the hardcover edition as follows:
Hughes, Dean, 1943-
Team player / by Dean Hughes.—1st ed.
p. cm.—(Scrappers; #3)
Summary: When Trent's best friend, Robbie, and another teammate on the Scrappers begin bragging about their baseball abilities, Trent worries that it will affect the team's play.
ISBN 0-689-81926-9 (hc)   0-689-81936-6 (pbk)
[1. Baseball—Fiction. 2. Teamwork (Sports)—Fiction. 3. Best friends—Fiction.]
I. Title. II. Series: Hughes, Dean, 1943-   Scrappers; #3
PZ7.H87312T1   1999
[Fic]-dc21   98-7907

CHAPTER ONE

"Mine! Mine!"

Trent Lubak trotted into left center field and waved Jeremy Lim off. He knew he might have to make a quick throw once he caught the ball, but still, he watched it all the way into his glove.

Smack! The ball thumped into the pocket, nice and solid. Only then did he look toward the infield.

The runner on second made a move toward third, so Trent pivoted toward Robbie Marquez and threw hard. The throw was like an arrow, right on target. The runner took a good look, checked up, and hurried back to second.

"Two away!" Gloria Gibbs yelled. She waved her fist with her index and pinky fingers sticking out like horns. Then she turned back toward Trent and gave him a thumbs-up.

"Nice catch, Trent!" Robbie yelled. "Way to be there."

It hadn't been a tough catch, so it was no big deal. But Trent was always relieved when he made a good play. Sometimes he wished he could hit the ball into the next county, like Wilson Love, or field ground balls like Gloria or Robbie. But he couldn't, so he just tried to be dependable and not let the team down.

When Trent and Robbie were younger, they had both been pretty good players. But in the last year or so, Robbie had improved a lot faster than Trent. Trent didn't have sprinter's speed like Robbie, and especially not like Thurlow Coates. Thurlow had more raw talent than anyone on the team, but he rode the bench most of the time. Coach Carlton just couldn't rely on the guy to give his full effort. Today Thurlow was in the starting lineup, in right field, but this was the first time all season.

"Chuck it in there, Ollie!" Gloria yelled. Her voice was like an air horn. If a guy stood next to her, he could get his eardrums broken. "Hit it right here, batta. I want *you!*"

"Knock it to me, Gunnarson," Robbie yelled. "I'm gonna gun you down."

"This glove *swallows* baseballs," Gloria shouted, more at Robbie than at the batter. "I'm the best there is. You don't believe it, try me."

Robbie seemed to think he had to answer that one. "*Nothing* gets by me. I'm Velcro man." He laughed and pounded his glove.

Trent didn't like to hear Robbie talking like that. He never used to. He seemed to be acting more like Gloria all the time lately.

Before the game Gloria had been telling everyone how good she was. "I'm batting four hundred. I hope you guys all know that," she told the other players—loud enough for everyone in the park to hear. "I thought you guys weren't going to let a girl show you up."

Gloria's friend Tracy Matlock laughed. She played second base and was a pretty good hitter herself. "Without us, these *boys* would be in trouble," she said. Cindy Jones, the other girl on the team, also laughed, but she didn't have a lot to brag about. So far, she hadn't been hitting very well.

The boys didn't say a word. Trent, for one, knew that Tracy was right. Gloria and Tracy were two of the best players on the team.

But Robbie told Gloria, "Hey, I'm batting

almost four hundred myself. And I'll make you a promise: No one is going to get me out today—not once. Let's see who's got the best average when the day is over."

"You're on," Gloria told him. "But let's also see who makes the all-star team when the season is over."

Robbie finally seemed to realize he had been sounding like a jerk. "Hey, I'm not claiming I'm some kind of superstar," he admitted, glancing at Trent. "I'm just saying I can hit this pitcher for the Whirlwinds."

So maybe Robbie wasn't as bad as Gloria. But Trent hated *all* this kind of talk. His dad always told him to do his job, play hard, and play smart. The best players spoke with their bats—and their gloves. Perhaps Robbie and Gloria were both better players than Trent was—but if they were, they didn't have to be the ones to say so.

In any case, the kid who was up to bat—Gary Gunnarson—didn't seem too worried about any of the stuff Gloria and Robbie were yelling. He waited on Ollie Allman's curveball, and he knocked a hard shot right between the two of them.

Trent took off as soon as he saw the ball dart toward the outfield, and he got to it quickly. He saw that the runner was charging hard toward third, looking like he was heading for home. Trent cocked his arm to make the throw, but he heard the Whirlwinds' coach shout, "Hold up!"

In that instant, Trent made an instant decision. He bluffed a throw home, saw that the runner really was holding, and then he spun toward second. Gunnarson had rounded first, clearly expecting to go to second on Trent's throw home. When he saw Trent turn to throw, however, he stopped.

Trent ran toward the infield. He watched both runners, but he didn't make a wild toss. The runners retreated to their bases, at first and third.

Trent had made a smart move—the kind that won games. He had stopped a run from scoring, had kept Gunnarson out of scoring position, and had kept the force play alive at second.

Coach Carlton noticed. "Good job, Trent," he shouted. "That's heads-up play."

"Still two away," Trent shouted. "Let's get this next guy." What he wanted to say was,

"Hey, Robbie and Gloria, keep your mouths shut and make a play this time." But Trent never popped off like that.

Trent didn't have to; over on first, Gunnarson was doing all the talking. "Hey, I thought you two were going to take anything I hit your way," he yelled at them. "Did the ball get by you just a little too fast? Did I hit it just a little too hard for you?"

For once Gloria kept her mouth shut.

And Robbie only called to Ollie, "Don't worry about the runners. Just throw strikes."

Ollie was being Ollie. He was pacing around the mound, talking to himself, looking strange. His long legs and his odd walk made him look more like a sandhill crane than a baseball pitcher.

When he finally stepped back to the pitching rubber, he stretched his neck and stared at Wilson Love, the catcher. Then his head bobbed as he accepted the signal.

He threw a fastball that stayed up in the strike zone. The batter got under the ball and lifted a little fly over Gloria's head. She turned and ran after it. As she did, she watched the ball over her shoulder and dug hard.

The ball was looping toward the gap between left and center. Jeremy was charging hard, but he seemed to have no chance to get to it.

Trent couldn't get there either, but he ran all out, at least hoping to cut the ball off quickly when it dropped.

When Gloria realized she had no play, she pulled up and shouted, "Yours, yours!" Then she crouched down to stay out of the way.

The ball was carrying longer than Trent had expected, and Jeremy wasn't giving up. The kid could fly, and he was closing in on the ball.

"Mine, mine!" Jeremy yelled, and at the last second, he dove.

He got his glove under the ball just before it hit the grass. But Jeremy hit the ground hard, and he rolled. As he did, the ball popped into the air.

Trent didn't know whether the ball had hit the ground or not. He had only seen it shoot into the air. But he knew he had to grab it fast, and Jeremy was stretched out on the ground in front of him.

Trent jumped over Jeremy and reached high in the air. The ball was at the top of its arc, seeming to float. Trent snagged it, landed just beyond Jeremy, and cocked his arm to throw. But just then he heard the umpire yell, "Oooooouuuuuut!"

The ball had come off Jeremy's glove and never touched the ground. The Scrappers were out of the inning—and no runs had scored.

Gloria grabbed Trent and slapped him on the back. Then Jeremy jumped up and started pounding on him, too. At the same time, Robbie charged from the infield. "Way to be there!" he yelled, and he gave Trent a big high five.

As Trent looked at the bleachers behind his team's bench, he could see that his parents, along with all the other Scrappers fans, were excited. They were clapping and yelling. He could even hear people shouting his name.

Trent liked all that—in a way. But that much attention also embarrassed him. He ducked his head and ran to the dugout. When he got there, it all started again. Each of the Scrappers had to give him a high five, or low five, or some other kind of five. Even Thurlow said, "Nice catch."

Trent thanked everyone, and then he tried to change the subject. "Okay, who's up?" he yelled. "Let's get some runs. We need to break this game open." Trent was not at all satisfied with a 6 to 3 lead at the end of the third inning. He knew how quickly that lead could disappear if Ollie started walking a lot of batters—as he often did.

Robbie and Trent were standing outside the dugout, near the bat rack. Robbie grabbed a bat. "Hey, I want your autograph, Mr. Golden Glove," he said. "Or is your name Griffey?"

Trent laughed. Robbie knew that Ken Griffey, Jr., was one of Trent's heroes. But Trent said, "It wasn't that hard a catch. Jeremy was the one who made the tough play to keep the ball alive."

"Yeah, but you were right where you had to be," Robbie said. "And that was some jump you made. Welcome to the Bigs, buddy." He gave his bat a couple of swings, and then he walked to the plate to lead off the inning.

Trent frowned. He liked the praise, but who was Robbie to be welcoming anybody to the "Bigs"?

What was with Robbie lately? When he had lost the competition to play shortstop—to Gloria, of all people—he had been down and discouraged. Now, no matter what he had told Gloria, the guy *did* seem to think he was a superstar.

Wilson walked by Trent on his way out to the on-deck circle. "Nice catch, man," he said, slapping Trent on the shoulder. "A lot of guys would have let up and just trotted over there. You kept right on going."

Trent hadn't realized the coach was behind them. "That's right," Coach Carlton said. "Trent is the hardest-working player on this team. It pays off, too. If everyone would put out the same way, no one in this league could beat us."

Trent turned around and looked at the coach. "Thanks," he said. Then he headed for the bench. He sat down by himself before anyone could embarrass him any more.

But he liked what Coach Carlton had called him: "the hardest-working player on the team." There was nothing wrong with that. Okay, so no one had ever called him a star, and chances were, no one ever would. But there was nothing he could do about that.

Trent watched Robbie take a nice cut at the first pitch—and miss. Then Robbie stepped out of the box, knocked his bat against his shoes, adjusted the sweatbands on his wrists, tugged on his cap, and stepped back to the plate.

Oh, brother. What was Robbie trying to do? Act like a major leaguer? Maybe Trent was better off not being a star. At least he had enough sense not to act like that.

Somebody really needed to tell Robbie to lay off all the showboat stuff. But Trent didn't think he dared do it. The two of them had been best friends forever, and Trent didn't want to say anything that would make Robbie mad.

CHAPTER TWO

Trent told himself to stop letting Robbie and Gloria bother him. The important thing was, the team had to come through. So when Robbie hit a stinger of a line drive past the second baseman, Trent jumped up and cheered for him.

The right fielder got to the ball quickly and made a good throw to second. Robbie had to stop at first.

As soon as he walked back to the bag, he yelled, "Hey, Gloria, that's three hits for me. My batting average must be higher than yours now."

Trent knew that Gloria only had one hit so far, but that didn't seem to worry her. She yelled across the diamond, "Three crummy little singles. And no runs batted in. I drove in two runs with my double."

"Gloria, I don't want to hear that," Coach

Carlton yelled to her. "Let's think about our won-lost record."

Wilson had stepped to the plate and taken his stance. He looked as awkward as ever, but he was hitting better lately—not hitting quite so many long balls, but not striking out so much either. Trent hoped he would lose one over the fence this time up. Two more runs might give the Scrappers the cushion they needed.

At the beginning of the season, the Whirlwinds had made the Scrappers look bad. It wasn't that they were so great; it was just that the Scrappers had had a hard time getting started.

The Whirlwinds' record was 2 and 2. They had fair pitching, fair hitting, fair everything—but *only* fair. Trent knew for sure that the Scrappers had more talent. They were just too inconsistent.

Still, the Scrappers had improved a lot in the past couple of weeks. After a big comeback against the Stingrays the week before, the players' confidence was growing. And everyone was getting along better than they had at first.

But Gloria and Robbie could end all that. Trent had noticed that he wasn't the only one getting tired of all the bragging. He had heard Tracy say, "What's with Robbie? We don't need two Glorias on this team. One is more than enough."

And Adam Pfitzer had told Trent, "I used to really like Robbie, but lately, I don't even want to be around him."

Trent hated to think what might happen to the team if too many of the players started saying things like that.

Wilson took some good swings, but he ended up lifting a high fly to left. The left fielder loped in a few steps, caught the ball, and then made a good throw to second to hold Robbie at first.

Thurlow walked to the plate. The guy was hard to figure. Every now and then he would show what a great player he was—would even seem to care. But now he stood at the plate like a guy hanging out on a street corner.

Chuck Kenny, the Whirlwinds' first baseman, was mouthing off as usual, but even that didn't seem to get Thurlow's attention.

Wilson walked into the dugout. He gave his batting helmet a toss and then dropped onto the bench next to Trent. "Man, I wanted to hit that ball a mile out of here. I probably swung too hard."

"I don't think so," Trent said. "You got under it a little, but it was a good swing."

Just then Thurlow came out of his relaxed stance and lashed a screaming line drive past the right fielder and into the corner. Trent and Wilson stood and cheered with the rest of the team. Robbie turned on the speed, raced all the way around third and scored. Thurlow cruised into second with a stand-up double.

"Man, if I could hit—and *run*—like either one of those guys, I'd never complain," Wilson said.

"I know what you mean," Trent agreed.

"Nice shot, Thurlow," Robbie was yelling as he trotted back toward the dugout.
Then he told Tracy, "You can hit this guy. He's losing his stuff."

The Whirlwinds were using a different pitcher from the one the Scrappers had faced earlier in the season. He was a stocky little guy, but he pumped the ball pretty hard. Trent didn't know him, but he had heard the Whirlwind players call him Bailey.

Robbie was practically bouncing as he came

into the dugout. "Four-run lead, gang. Let's keep building it. It feels good to be in front for a change."

Gloria walked over and slapped hands with him. "Just wait until I get up," she said. "I'll put the game away."

"Hey, I'm the one on the hot streak," Robbie said. "Just get on my back and *ride*."

Gloria only laughed. She walked out and got a bat, and then she crouched in the on-deck circle. "I'm going deep with the ball this time," she yelled back at Robbie.

But all the talk came to nothing. Tracy grounded out to the pitcher, and Thurlow had to hold at second. Then Gloria popped out. So after a great start to the fourth inning, the Scrappers got only one run. The score was 7 to 3, but there was still a long way to go.

"Okay," Coach Carlton told the kids, "let's play some defense. Martin, you're in for Trent. Chad, you're in for Thurlow. Let's go!"

Trent had been heading out of the dugout. He turned around and walked back to the bench. He understood that the coach wanted everyone to play, but if he was the hardest-working guy on the team, why was he also the first one to get pulled—along with a guy who didn't seem to care?

"Well . . . I guess we get some pine time," Trent told Thurlow.

"Whatever. It doesn't matter to me." It was Thurlow's usual answer. Trent figured the coach had tried to fire up Thurlow by letting him start today. That was probably a reward for Thurlow's good play against the Stingrays. Thurlow had played well today, too. But his attitude was right back where it usually was.

"That was a nice stroke, Thurlow," Trent said. "You have about the quickest swing I've ever seen."

Thurlow shrugged and looked away.

Trent decided not to talk to the guy. What a team this was. The best players were all acting like a bunch of jerks.

And speaking of jerks, Chuck Kenny was leading off the inning for the Whirlwinds. He told Ollie, "This is your last inning. We're knocking you out. And I'm going to land the first blow."

He kept his promise. Ollie threw a decent

fastball, but Chuck pounded it hard to left field. Martin Epting could have held the hit to a single, but he was slow getting over, and the ball got past him. Chuck ended up with a double.

Ollie walked the next batter, and then the catcher came up and drove a fly to right. Chad Corrigan seemed to have it all the way, but the ball hit his glove and popped back out. Now the bases were loaded.

"Oh, man," Trent muttered. "I wish the coach had left us in one more inning." But when he looked over at Thurlow, the guy was leaning back with his eyes shut. Trent doubted he was really asleep, but he didn't say a word.

But just when disaster seemed to be sneaking up on the Scrappers, the Whirlwinds' third baseman slapped a grounder to Tracy. Tracy made a good pickup and a good throw to second. Gloria hustled to the bag, took the throw, and then gunned the ball to first for the double play.

One run scored, but now there were two outs. Things were looking better.

Another run scored when Ollie threw a wild pitch high, but the next batter rolled a grounder toward Adam at first base. Adam tagged the runner for the final out, and Trent took a deep breath of relief. At least the Scrappers still had a two-run lead, 7 to 5.

But Gloria was at it again. "Robbie, it's a good thing that was my play. You never could have completed that double play," she told him. "I have a rifle for an arm, and you have a peashooter."

"No way. I would have had the guy, easy," Robbie said. "This is a *cannon*." He flexed his muscle.

"Somebody shut those two up," Jeremy whispered to Trent. And Jeremy never said anything bad about anyone.

Ollie came up first in the top of the fifth inning. He obviously wanted those runs back. He swung way too hard and struck out on three pitches.

Martin came up next, filling Trent's spot at the bottom of the order. Martin was actually hitting pretty well at practice these days, but he seemed to get too nervous when he got in a game. He fouled two away. Then he swung early on a curveball and also struck out.

That brought up Jeremy. Jeremy had gone

three for three today already—and he hadn't said a word about it.

On the first pitch, he crunched one right over the pitcher's mound. Bailey was still off balance when he stuck out his glove to stop the ball. It nicked the fingers of his glove and deflected toward left field.

The shortstop had been running toward the hole at second when the ball suddenly careened behind him. Jeremy was on for the fourth time.

Up came Adam, swinging his bat as he walked to the plate. He settled in, then watched the first pitch sail wide.

Trent thought Bailey's motion was starting to look a little stiff. Maybe he was getting tired. After he threw ball four, he stepped away from the pitcher's mound and started rubbing his shoulder.

The Whirlwinds' coach trotted out to the mound. He chatted with Bailey for a few seconds and then called to Chuck to come over from first to pitch to Robbie. A sub came in to play first, and Bailey walked to the bench.

Chuck took a few warm-up pitches, and then he walked halfway to home plate and said, "Robbie, you aren't even going to *see* the ball, let alone hit it."

"I'll *see* it until it drops over the fence," Robbie told him. "Then you'll have to go *look* for it."

"That's enough, boys," the ump said. "Let's play ball."

Two on, two out. Trent knew that Robbie wanted this bad, and that worried him. Maybe Robbie would try too hard to hit the long ball he had promised.

Robbie took a nasty fastball at the knees for a strike and then another blazer up high for a ball.

But the next pitch was belt high, and Robbie unloaded on it. He slashed a ball in the right center gap that got past the fielders and rolled to the fence. Both runs scored. Now Robbie had four hits for the day and he had driven in as many runs as Gloria.

Trent could hardly believe how good the guy was. Somehow, being the hardest worker on the team didn't seem like such a big deal anymore.

But now Robbie was strutting around like he was the new Joe DiMaggio. Trent sort of wished Robbie would get picked off—or fall on his face rounding third. Something needed to bring him down to earth.

Wilson came up next and finally got himself a nice hit—a single that drove in Robbie. When the inning ended, the Scrappers had a five-run lead, with the score at 10 to 5.

The Whirlwinds were turning into the Gentle Breeze right before the Scrappers' eyes. Ollie was throwing strikes, and the Whirlwinds were all trying to get back into the game with big hits. They went down one-two-three in the bottom of the fifth, and Chuck got the only Whirlwind hit the rest of the day. The Scrappers picked up two more runs in the sixth, when Chad and Cindy walked, and—after Jeremy finally made an out—Adam sent a long shot to the fence in right.

So the final score was 12 to 5. The Scrappers seemed happy about the win, but the players separated quickly and took off in all directions. Trent didn't like the feel of that.

Robbie was still excited. "Man, what a day I had!" he told Trent. "Gloria's not saying much now, is she?"

"Nope," was all Trent said.

Robbie seemed to sense what Trent was thinking. "Hey, but that was a great catch you made. We needed a big play right then, and you came through with it."

Trent nodded.

"Well . . . I better go find my parents. They're waiting for me."

"Okay. I'll see you later," Trent said.

"Do you want to get together—hang out or something?"

"Uh . . . I don't think so. I've got some things I've got to do."

"Okay. Well, let's meet in the morning and work out for a while."

"All right."

Trent took a deep breath and walked away. He really didn't like the way he was feeling. He knew he felt bad about not getting any hits— and getting pulled from the game. But that was nothing new. What bothered him most was the way he was feeling about his best friend.

CHAPTER THREE

Early the next morning Trent was sitting in the bleachers at the field waiting for Robbie to show up. The two liked to work out together before the day got hot. But today Robbie was late.

Trent heard the sound of a bike pulling up to a stop behind him, but when he looked through the metal benches, it was Wilson he saw, not Robbie. Wilson and some of the other players sometimes showed up for these little workouts, too.

Wilson dropped his bike and walked around to Trent. "Where's Robbie?" he asked.

"I don't know. Sometimes he doesn't wake up. About half the time lately, I end up over here by myself."

"I guess maybe Robbie doesn't need to practice," Wilson said. He laughed. "To hear him tell it, he's as good as he needs to be."

"Yeah. Him and Gloria both."

"Everyone on the team is getting tired of those two. Tracy is *sick* of Gloria—and they're supposed to be best friends."

"I think even Thurlow was getting mad about it yesterday."

"Mad? He told me he was going to have it out with Robbie, if he doesn't lay off."

"I don't get it, Wilson. Robbie's never been like that. And now—just when the team starts to play some decent ball together—he's getting everybody mad again."

"Why don't you say something to him about it? You're his best friend."

"I've been thinking I should. But I don't know exactly what to tell him."

Wilson laughed again. "Tell him, 'You better keep your mouth shut or Thurlow's going to beat your head in.'"

"Hey, that would make *me* listen," Trent said. He laughed, too, but this whole thing wasn't that funny to him. He didn't want the other players mad at Robbie. No matter how upset Trent had been with him lately, the guy had still been his best friend since the two were just little kids.

"Not that Thurlow has any room to talk,"

Wilson said. "He still doesn't care whether we win or lose. He gets up there and hits the ball—just to show he can do it. And then he plunks himself down on the bench and says, 'So what?'"

"I know. What's with him? Last week he was starting to act like he wanted to play." Trent had slipped his glove on, and now he pounded his fist into the pocket.

"I heard him jawing with his mom again before the game," Wilson said. "Every time he gets mad at her, he takes it out on the team."

Trent stood up and took a look around. He couldn't see Robbie—or anyone else—heading for the field. "If we could get everyone playing at the same time, we'd be unstoppable," he said.

"Do you think that will ever happen?"

"To tell you the truth, I doubt it."

Trent sat down again, and the two stared off toward Mount Timpanogos. The snow was melting off fast these days, but up toward the top there was one field of snow that stayed year-round. Trent had climbed the peak a couple of times and then slid down "the glacier," as everyone called it. It had been a wild ride, with nothing but a plastic bag for a sled.

Last summer Trent and Robbie had made the hike up "Timp" together. It crossed Trent's mind that they ought to do something like that again. Maybe it would give them a chance to talk things over.

"You wanna throw the ball around?" Wilson asked.

"Sure."

The two got up. For a time they tossed the ball easily, but gradually they moved farther apart and started to put a little heat on their throws.

"Is your arm warm yet?" Wilson asked.

"Yeah."

"Why don't you go out and cover the bag, and I'll practice my throw to second."

"All right," Trent said, and then he tried to imitate Gloria's foghorn voice. "I'll handle anything you can throw me."

Wilson shook his head. "Don't do that. It's too early in the morning to hear that voice."

Trent trotted to second base, but he felt a little awkward. He wasn't used to playing the infield. "What do you want me to do?"

"For now, just stand there. Maybe we'll get tricky in a minute."

Wilson crouched down behind home plate,

then jumped up into a throwing position and fired the ball toward second. Trent flinched just a little as the ball smacked into the heel of his glove, but he tried not to show that it had hurt. He pretended to make the tag, and then he threw the ball hard, back to Wilson.

Again, Wilson jumped up and fired, and this time Trent was better prepared. He made the catch, then pretended to throw the ball to first. They did this a few more times before Wilson said, "Okay. Let's take the next step. You play off the bag, and when you cut to second, I'll hit you."

So Trent set up a few yards away from second, then charged toward the base. He got there well ahead of the ball, but Wilson hit the spot about right. After a few more tries and a couple of trips into the outfield to chase the ball down, Trent and Wilson had timed it out pretty well.

"Okay, back up," Wilson yelled. "Let's see what your arm is made of."

Trent backpedaled into shallow left field, and then he threw the ball hard to the plate. Wilson had to stand up to make the catch. "Good arm! But get it to me on one nice hop, the way you're supposed to."

Trent threw it in from shallow left several times. Once he started getting the one-hoppers just right, he backed up more and tried again. After fifteen minutes or so, he was standing at a medium depth in left, throwing the ball toward an imaginary cutoff man.

The idea was to throw at the cutoff, hard and fairly low. If the catcher called for the ball to go through, it should bounce once and come up nicely for the catcher to handle. But if the catcher saw no chance for a play at home, he would yell, "Cut!" and the cutoff man would catch it and try to make a play on a runner. A good throw was not easy. It took not only a lot of power, but also near-perfect accuracy.

A guy needed to know what he could do, too. From deep in the outfield, he had no chance to make a good throw all the way to the plate. That's when the cutoff player moved toward the outfielder and gave him a target. The cutoff would take the throw and then pivot and fire the ball home—or to one of the bases if it was too late to make a play at the plate.

After so many throws, Trent's arm was getting tired. "One more," he shouted. He took a hopping half step toward the bag to get his whole body into the throw. He watched the ball as it left his hand and traveled in a shallow arc—right at the cutoff man he was imagining—and bounced to Wilson.

Just right!

Trent jogged toward Wilson with a smile on his face.

"Hey, that was a great throw," Wilson said, as Trent came near. "You da man."

"No," Trent said. "You da man."

"No, you da man."

"No, you . . ." By then both boys were laughing.

They walked across the infield and sat down on the front row of the bleachers. Neither one wanted to throw any more and get their arms too sore. But they decided to wait to see whether anyone else showed up. Sometimes Martin and Chad or even Gloria and Tracy would come over. Trent had brought a bat, and he wanted to do some hitting, but there was no way for two guys—with one ball—to hold batting practice.

"So what's the deal between you and Robbie?" Wilson asked. "You sound like you're pretty mad at him."

"No. I'm not mad. I just hate all the big talk. And the way he's showboating when he's up to bat. Stuff like that. I'm still his friend. I just hate to see him acting so stupid."

"You gotta admit, though—he's good. And so is Gloria."

"I know that. That doesn't bother me. It's not like I think I'm as good as they are. I just don't want to hear them talking about it all the time."

Wilson nodded.

"A guy should go out there and do his job," Trent said. "If he's good, everyone will see it."

"The worst part is, they may be good, but they make it sound like they're a couple of pros."

"Yeah. Did you hear them yesterday?" In a voice imitating Robbie's, Trent said, "Hey, Gloria, did you see me make that impossible stop, that perfect throw, that . . . blah, blah, blah."

Wilson laughed, and in a booming "Gloria voice" said, "Did you see me catch that grounder with my bare hand—and toss it over my shoulder to second?"

"Oh, yeah?" Trent said, still trying to sound

like Robbie. "Well, I dove for one and caught it with my teeth, then spit it all the way to first."

"That's nothing. I'm so fast that I once played shortstop in two games at the same time."

"Well, I'm so good that I played third and short at the same time."

"I played shortstop and center field."

"I played pitcher *and* catcher."

The two were both laughing hard by then. Wilson's imitation of Gloria was almost perfect. "I played the entire infield," he claimed.

And Trent's imitation of Robbie was just as good. "Puh-lease! I played third while selling hot dogs in the bleachers."

They were both cracking up . . . when they heard a voice behind them.

"You guys are really funny, you know that?"

Trent and Wilson spun around and looked through the bleachers. There was Robbie sitting on his bike.

Trent felt sick.

"If you've got a problem with me, why don't you say it to my face?"

"Robbie," Trent started, but he couldn't

think of anything to say. "We were just . . . kidding around."

"You guys just don't have anything to brag about. That's your problem. Every time we get something going, one of you strikes out and ends the inning."

"Hey, come on. Don't start that," Wilson said. "We were just—"

"I thought you guys were my friends. Now I know the truth." Robbie gave a push with his foot and pedaled off on his bike. Wilson and Trent just watched him go.

"Oh, man," Trent whispered. "I can't believe that happened." He bent forward and put his head in his hands.

CHAPTER FOUR

Trent thought about following Robbie home and telling him he was sorry. But what was he supposed to say? "Yeah, we were putting you down, but . . ."

Trent really couldn't come up with a good way to finish that sentence. He knew he should be honest with Robbie—tell him why the players were mad at him. But that wasn't going to be easy—especially now that Robbie was so mad.

On the following morning the team had an official practice. Trent hoped he would get a chance to patch things up. But it was clear from the beginning that Robbie wanted nothing to do with him. Every time the two got close to each other, Robbie made a point of walking away.

The whole team seemed to feel the tension.

The word had gotten around about what had happened, and most of the players seemed to be on Trent and Wilson's side. Tracy even told Trent, "I'm glad Robbie heard you guys. Maybe it will do some good. I just wish Gloria had been there."

But Gloria had heard the story, too, and she had her own point of view. She marched up to Trent and said, "Hey, Trent—Mr. Number Nine Batter—if you've got a problem with me, tell me to my face, right now."

"Look, Gloria," Trent said, "we were just—"

"Just dissing me behind my back—that's what you were doing."

"Not exactly."

"Yeah. *Exactly*."

Trent thought about telling her what they had actually said, and why. But she wasn't about to listen.

"You talk that way about me again, and I'll reach down your throat and rip your tongue out. And don't think I can't do it." She poked Trent in the chest with her finger, glared at him for a few seconds, and walked away.

Trent let her go. He felt like an idiot, but he didn't want to get into a big argument—or a fist-fight—and watch the team fall apart again. As it turned out, though, his choice didn't make any difference. All during practice he watched the players whispering or talking in little groups. The team was actually as divided as it had ever been—or more so.

Wilson told Trent, "Well . . . at least those two aren't bragging today." But Trent almost wished they were. That had to be better than everyone angry with one another.

The team would be playing the Mustangs in a couple of days. The Mustangs were the only team in the league that hadn't lost a game. The Scrappers had given them about as good a fight as anyone so far, and since then they had been playing better all the time. But it was hard to say what might happen now.

At the end of practice Coach Carlton called the players together. The kids sat down on the grass while he talked to them. "Listen, I'm feeling something strange here," he said. "Who wants to tell me what's going on?"

No one said a word. Trent glanced over at

Robbie, who looked away. Trent had a feeling it would only make things worse if he tried to explain things to the coach.

"Well, I don't get it," the coach said. "I thought we came together in that last game. Some good things started to happen. But today you all look like a bunch of sleepwalkers. You don't act like you even care about baseball."

Again, no one spoke.

"Look, kids, we've got a tough game this week. I'd really like to beat the Mustangs after what they did to us last time. Do you remember how cocky those kids were with their fancy uniforms and their loud mouths? Wouldn't you like to shut them up?"

Coach had never said anything like that before. Trent could tell he was looking for some way to fire up the team. But not much happened. Some of the players said, "Yeah," but there was no excitement in their voices.

"What do you say we have an extra practice tomorrow morning? Let's get ready for these guys," Coach Carlton said, raising his voice a little.

"Yeah. Let's do it!" Gloria said. Then she stood up and looked around at the other players.

"Some of you think I brag too much," she said. "Well, here's what I have to say. You play as good as me, and you can brag, too. I don't care whether we're all lovey-dovey on this team. I just want to kick some butt. *Mustang* butt!"

That actually got a pretty good cheer. But Coach Carlton said, "Wait a minute. We don't need to start acting like the Mustangs. We just need to play some good baseball."

"Whatever. I still say we kick some butt!"

Again, all the kids cheered, and their enthusiasm carried over into practice the next morning. But Trent saw the problem. Maybe everyone disliked the Mustangs—and that seemed to bring about some unity. But if the players still disliked one another, he felt sure that sooner or later the team would break down again.

Trent knew he had to set things right with Robbie, but Robbie still wasn't giving him a chance.

On Friday, before the game started, Coach Carlton told the kids, "Okay, let's have some fun. Play smart, and remember the things we've been working on. We can beat these guys."

Everyone circled around, joined hands, and yelled, "GO SCRAPPERS!"

It seemed as though all the bad feelings had been forgotten. But when Trent tried to wish Robbie good luck, Robbie quickly turned away.

The Scrappers took the field first. Adam threw his final warm-up pitches, and then Wilson sent the ball around the horn as the Mustangs' leadoff batter stepped up to the plate.

Trent, far off in left field, was really nervous. The Mustangs were already making fun of the Scrappers, talking smack, bragging about how many runs they were going to score off Adam. Their fancy uniforms—black and white— looked all cleaned and pressed. The Scrappers' rust-colored T-shirts looked pretty sad by comparison.

Trent didn't have to wait long to get into the action. The first batter for the Mustangs, a muscular little kid named Billy Mauer, took a couple of pitches and then cracked a high fly to left.

Easy . . . easy . . . Trent told himself as he coasted under the ball. He waited, kept his eye on it, and then used both hands to close the glove and squeeze the ball.

He sighed with relief, and some of his nervousness disappeared. He tossed the ball to Gloria and then held up one finger. "One away. Way to chuck, Adam," he shouted.

"Good catch, Trent," Gloria yelled back at him.

But Robbie didn't even look at Trent. Trent told himself not to think about that. He would just do his job and hope everyone else did the same.

Adam should have had some confidence after getting the first batter, but maybe all the Mustangs' talk was bothering him. He had trouble finding the strike zone, and he walked the next two batters.

The cleanup hitter, a lefty, dug in at the plate and got ready. This was Alan Pingree, the big first baseman for the Mustangs. He was a big hitter—and an even bigger talker.

Both the infield and the outfield shifted toward the right field side. Trent only took a few steps to his left. Pingree was a good hitter and smart enough not to try to pull everything off a fast pitcher like Adam. Trent had seen the guy go to the opposite field with outside pitches.

As if in response to Trent's thoughts, Pingree

jumped on the first pitch and poked it toward third base, close to the left field line. Robbie took a couple of quick steps and dove. He didn't field the ball cleanly, but he knocked it down.

He jumped up, grabbed the ball, and then threw off balance toward first.

Trent knew what Robbie was thinking—that there was no chance at second or third, but that Pingree was slow. But the fact was, Robbie didn't have a chance of getting him.

The ball was not only late; it whizzed past Ollie's outstretched glove and bounced to the fence. A run scored, and the other runners ended up on second and third.

As Trent walked back to his position, he was mad. The old Robbie would have been smarter than to try to pull off a hotdog play like that. This all had to do with trying to show Gloria how strong his arm was.

When Trent looked back toward the infield, he could see that Robbie knew that, too. He was looking at the ground, then at the sky, everywhere but at the other players. Trent hoped he'd get his head on straight now. Maybe a dumb mistake, early, would actually be good for him.

And even though Trent didn't like to admit it

to himself, he sort of enjoyed seeing Robbie mess up for once. Sure, Robbie was good—but not so *great* as he had started to think he was.

But when the next batter singled and pushed across another run, Trent worried that the Mustangs were going to build a big lead—and the Scrappers would never have a chance.

Adam settled down, though. He came through with a tough srikeout on the next batter. Then, with two outs and runners at the corners, a guy Trent knew from school came up to bat—a kid everyone called "Gomer."

Trent knew the guy was sort of a hick—and maybe earned his nickname—but he was a good athlete. Trent backed up a few steps and waved Jeremy back. Thurlow was in right field, but he was paying no attention. He stayed where he was.

Trent just hoped Gomer didn't tag one. A two-run lead was something the Scrappers might come back from, but if Gomer smacked a dinger and gave the Mustangs a five-run lead, this game could be over before it got started.

When Gomer chased two pretty good pitches for strikes, Trent started to feel better. But then Adam tried to throw a curve and left it hanging over the plate. Gomer smashed it to right center.

Jeremy ran hard, but the ball was clearly over his head. The hit was going to go for extra bases, and at least two runs were going to score. Trent took off toward third to back up Robbie, but he kept watching Jeremy as he ran.

Suddenly Thurlow seemed to come out of nowhere—flying!

He was also too late. Trent could see that he couldn't get there in time either. But he leaped. He sailed into the air, up and up, like Michael Jordan, like there was some invisible wire pulling him higher, then holding him there. He reached across his body with his left hand and—as though it were easy—picked that ball out of the air.

Only then, it seemed to Trent, did Thurlow give his body permission to come back to earth.

Trent heard something like a gasp come out of the crowd, heard the same sound come out of himself. He had thought he was aware of what Thurlow could do. He knew the guy was a good athlete. But this was the first time Trent really understood. Thurlow was going to play in the majors someday.

Or at least he could—if he ever decided he wanted to.

Without thinking about what he was doing, Trent turned to the closest Scrapper to him, Robbie. "Did I just see what I think I did?" he asked.

"He's the same age we are," Robbie said. "How can he do that?"

For an instant it felt as though all the hard feelings were gone between them, but Robbie caught himself. He turned and ran back to the dugout.

Trent listened to the screaming coming from the bleachers and from the other Scrappers. He heard some of the excitement the team had been missing lately. "Now let's get some runs!" everyone was yelling. "Get some runners on base—and Thurlow can bring them home."

Thurlow strolled back to the dugout as though nothing had happened. Some of the players wanted to give him high fives, but Thurlow pretended not to notice. He walked on into the dugout and sat down.

Jeremy got a bat and walked to the plate to lead off. He wasn't one to do a lot of yelling, but

Trent saw how determined he was to get things going.

The Mustangs' pitcher—Derek Salinas—had a good fastball, but he didn't try to pitch to spots. He would usually smoke it down the middle and expect no one to hit it. But Jeremy waited for the right pitch, and then he timed his swing perfectly. He stroked a hot shot past the second baseman.

Jeremy should have pulled up for a single, but he ignored Wanda Coates—Thurlow's mom and the Scrappers' assistant coach. She was screaming at Jeremy to stop as he rounded second and kept digging. The play at second was close, but he slid in under the tag.

It had been a huge risk, but it had worked. The Scrappers were all the more excited.

"That's the stuff," Gloria shouted to him from the dugout. "Let's run these guys into the ground."

The rest of the Scrappers were screaming, too. But Trent heard Coach Carlton's voice above them. "Jeremy, when a coach tells you to stop at first, you stop. Do you hear me?"

Jeremy nodded his head. But he was grinning.

It was Trent who took the words to heart.

Some guys were like Thurlow. They had the talent to do almost anything they wanted. Other guys had to use their heads. Trent knew that was the kind of guy he was.

The team was the same way. The Scrappers had some good talent, but not enough to blow everyone away. They all had to play their best— and play together. It helped a lot if they felt good about one another, too, the way they did right now.

CHAPTER FIVE

The Scrappers were on fire. Everyone was stroking the ball. Wilson knocked a three-run homer in the first inning. Then in the second, a whole string of singles brought in another four runs.

Adam gave up one more run to the Mustangs in the second, but at the end of two innings, the Scrappers were up 7 to 3.

Neither team scored in the third, even though the Scrappers continued to hit the ball on the nose. But then, in the fourth, the Scrappers' old problems began to show up again.

Jeremy dropped a pop fly in short center, and then Ollie let a ground ball get past him at first base. It went for a double and put runners at second and third. Suddenly Adam, who had been solid since the first inning, lost his control again.

It was one of those nightmare innings when Adam couldn't find the plate, or when he did, the Scrappers' defense couldn't come through. The big blow was a double by Pingree that cleared the loaded bases.

The worst part was, Trent had a chance to catch the ball. If he had gotten just a little better jump on it, he might have made the play. But he couldn't make himself any faster.

He hadn't made an error or even a mental mistake. But when he thought of what a guy like Thurlow would have done, it was hard for Trent to have much faith in himself.

When the top of the inning ended, the Mustangs had scored six runs and were back in the lead, 9 to 7.

The score stayed the same in the fifth, but in the sixth the Scrappers got something going again. Trent got his first hit of the day—finally!—to lead off the inning. He lucked out a little by dropping a fly ball in front of the left fielder, who had probably been playing too deep.

Gloria was really riding Salinas, and she finally

seemed to get to him. He walked Ollie and Jeremy, and then he forced a pitch over the plate to Robbie. Robbie hit a *hot* line drive into the left center gap. Three runs scored, and Robbie ended up on third.

Gloria was coming up to bat, and she was feeling cocky now. "Hey, Robbie," she yelled, "you could have left a few guys out there. How can I drive anyone in if you clear the bases?"

"Just drive *me* home," Robbie called back to her. "We need the run."

Trent was walking back to the dugout after scoring. He met Wilson, who was on his way to the plate. "Maybe we've shut up Robbie a little anyway," Wilson said. "Gloria never will change."

"Let's not worry about all that right now," Trent said. "Let's just keep hitting the ball."

And that's what Gloria did. She pounded the ball hard on the ground, past the shortstop. Robbie scored from third, and the Scrappers had a two-run lead, 11 to 9.

When Gloria pulled up at first, Trent saw her jaw going, could even hear her voice all the way in the dugout. He couldn't understand much, but he did pick up something about "dead meat," and he knew that's what she was calling the Mustangs.

All Trent could think was, *Don't get them mad. That's not going to help us.*

The trouble was, Martin and Cindy were now playing, and the bottom half of the Scrappers' lineup wasn't that strong. Wilson did get a single, but then Martin hit into a surefire double play. And Cindy struck out.

What looked like a possible giant inning was over, and now the Scrappers had to play some serious defense.

Trent was just happy he was still in the game. Today, the coach had pulled Jeremy from center and Tracy from second. Trent and Thurlow were staying in this time. So far, Chad was still on the bench. So Trent still might be the next to go.

Coach Carlton had decided Adam had had enough for the day, so he asked Ollie to finish out the game. Trent wondered whether that was a good idea. Ollie seemed to get nervous when he had to start pitching in a tight situation.

Trent was worried himself when he watched Ollie pace and talk to himself. He couldn't hear Ollie from so far away, but the guy looked upset.

At the same time, the Mustangs were really working Ollie over, and Gloria and Pingree were shouting back and forth, the way they had all day. The coach kept telling Gloria to lay off, and she would for a few minutes; but after Pingree zinged her a few times, she would go after him again.

Trent didn't like the confusion, and he didn't think a two-run lead was big enough. But at least the Scrappers weren't getting on one another. They were concentrating on beating the Mustangs.

When Ollie couldn't manage to throw a strike to the first batter, however, Trent looked around and saw that his teammates were getting *very* antsy.

By the time the batter walked, Trent was so tense he was ready to eat his glove. Ollie was telling himself what an idiot he was—loud enough for Trent to hear now—and the Mustangs were all agreeing.

But Ollie did throw a strike to the next batter. The guy hit a rocket toward third base. Robbie dove and knocked the ball down, but he had no chance to make a play at first.

At least he kept his cool and didn't try to

make a late throw to second. And once again, he kept his mouth shut.

Gloria was now screaming, "That's it, Ollie. Throw strikes. We can handle anything they can hit."

He did make a good pitch, and the batter knocked a high fly to center. Martin was out there, and Trent held his breath. But Martin got under it and made the catch.

The only problem was, the runners knew Martin had a weak arm, and they both tagged up and took off. Martin should have had an easy out at second, but he looped a rainbow of a throw, and the runner slid in safe.

The tying runs were now in scoring position and there was only one out.

Trent knew who was coming up, though. Pingree.

Trent actually felt sick to his stomach. Adam hadn't gotten Pingree out all day, and Ollie wasn't likely to do a lot better.

The players on both sides, and the people in the crowd, were all raising the roof, but Trent kept everything inside. He hoped the ball would come his way—or Thurlow's—if it was a fly.

Trent didn't shift at all this time. Pingree had sprayed the ball around the field, but he hadn't pulled it all day.

Pingree let one pitch go by, and then—*slam!*—he stroked the next pitch to left, down the line, just as he had earlier in the game. This one was over Robbie's head, however, and heading toward the corner of the field.

Trent took off on an angle. He had no chance to catch the ball in the air, but he hoped to cut it off, hold Pingree at second, and keep the tying run at third.

He ran for all he was worth, glad that he hadn't shifted away from the line. He stretched out and lunged to snag the ball . . . but it bounced on by him and rolled toward the fence.

Two runs would score now. There was nothing he could do to stop that, but he had to get the ball back to the infield as fast as he could, to stop Pingree. By the time he chased the ball down, it had rolled up against the fence. He grabbed it bare-handed, with his back to the infield.

As he turned, he was planning to hit his cutoff man, but he realized that Pingree was almost to third base, and the Mustangs' coach was waving him home. They were going for broke, trying for an inside-the-park homer.

As Trent's arm moved forward, he was changing his mind as to what to do. He had nothing to lose, he realized; he might as well try to throw all the way home. But he hadn't gotten his feet set as well as he needed to, and the ball took off on him.

What he saw was almost unbelievable. The ball sailed fairly far, but on a crazy angle, off over the fence along the third base line. It was heading for the bleachers, not home plate.

Trent never saw it land. He turned around and ducked his head. He heard the Mustangs erupt with joy as Pingree scored. They were ahead again, 12 to 11.

When Trent finally turned around, Gloria was staring at him with her hands on her hips. She wasn't yelling, but she looked disgusted. Robbie was looking toward home plate, and he was hammering his fist into his glove.

The Mustang players were the ones nice enough to let Trent know what a loser he was. "Now try this field over here," someone yelled.

Trent felt his face redden. It hadn't just been

a bad throw; it had been some sort of misfire. The Mustangs had the lead, and all the confidence, too. But for Trent the worst part was knowing he had made a stupid play—something he could have avoided. The throw hadn't been the mistake either. The mistake had been trying to cut the ball off too shallow.

He *knew* his own abilities. He knew how little speed he had. He should have angled back more, not attempted to cut the ball off quite so quickly. He would have given up two runs that way, but he wouldn't have allowed Pingree to circle the bases and score.

Trent watched, feeling numb, as the next batter grounded out to Adam. The third out came on an infield pop-up to Cindy.

Maybe the Scrappers could scrap their way back again. But Trent's confidence was gone. He hoped the coach would put Chad in, so he wouldn't have to bat again.

He jogged to the dugout, trying to look at no one. When he reached the bench, he saw Robbie come toward him, and he thought for a moment that his best buddy was going to tell him not to worry about his mistake.

But Robbie's eyes were cold as stones.

"What kind of a throw was that? I was out there waiting, and you didn't even try to get the ball to me."

"It was too late for that. I had to go all the way home."

"Is that what you call it? Home?"

"The ball got away from me. I—" But Trent stopped. Several of the Scrappers were standing behind Robbie, and they looked upset, too—as though Trent were the only guy who had ever made a bad play. Suddenly he stopped caring about fixing things with Robbie, stopped caring about team unity—or anything else. He just wanted Robbie to *shut up*.

"What about that throw you made in the first inning?" he suddenly shouted into Robbie's face. "You tell me. What was *that* about?"

"I just made a bad throw. Anyone can—"

"No. You threw the ball when it was already too late. You should have held on to it. My only chance was to let fly with the ball. I had nothing to lose."

"No way!" Robbie shouted back, and they were nose to nose now. "If you had hit me with a good throw, I still might have thrown him out. *That* was our only shot."

"Well, at least I saved us from that. If you *had* made this great throw you're *dreaming* about, we would have heard about it forever." Trent turned, walked to the far end of the bench, and sat down.

Robbie took a step toward Trent, as though he were going to chase him down, but Wilson grabbed his shoulder. "Leave him alone," Wilson said. "You know he's right."

Tracy was right there, too, pushing Robbie in the chest. "We've heard about enough from you, Robbie. Get off Trent's back."

Of course Gloria couldn't miss this kind of action. She started chewing at Tracy, and suddenly everyone was pushing and shouting. It was hard, in the confusion, even to know which side anyone was on.

The coach ran into the dugout and pulled Wilson and Robbie apart. "Sit down, everyone," he told the kids. "What in the world do you think you're doing?"

Everyone did sit down, but they all looked angry. No one was cheering for Adam, who was walking out to lead off the inning.

Nothing changed in the final inning. Trent came up with a chance to drive in the tying run, but he hit a soft roller to second base, and that was that.

The Scrappers lost the game 12 to 11.

When the game ended, the coach called the players together, but Trent only heard that from a distance. He was already clearing out. He avoided everyone, including his parents, and he walked home alone. Once he got there, he went to his room and closed the door behind him.

CHAPTER SIX

Trent never wanted to leave his room again. And he certainly didn't want anyone coming in. But he hadn't been home more than a few minutes when someone knocked at the door.

Trent knew it was either his dad or his mom—or both—and he felt like telling them to leave him alone. But he walked to the door and opened it. It was his dad.

"Look," Trent said, "I just want to—"

"Feel sorry for yourself?"

"No." Trent turned and walked away from the door. He sat down on his bed.

His dad walked in, got Trent's desk chair, turned it toward Trent, and sat down. "The ball slipped out of your hand, Trent. That's the whole story. There was no reason to run and hide when the game was over. The coach had some good things to say."

Mr. Lubak was a quiet man who hardly ever lectured Trent or chewed him out. But he could put him in his place when he felt he had to. Trent knew he was going to get a speech now—and he didn't want that. His dad obviously didn't understand what had gone on out there.

"Dad," Trent said, "it wasn't just the throw. Everything went wrong after that."

"Hey, I wasn't that far away. I saw what happened between you and Robbie."

Mr. Lubak was a manager at a company that made software for computers. He liked to solve problems, work things out; but he seemed to think kids could work things out the way employees at a company would. Trent doubted that would work with the Scrappers. "You don't know the whole story," he told his dad.

Trent's dad leaned forward and put his elbows on his knees. He was a tall man, and when he bent over like that, he seemed all arms and legs. Right now, though, his steady eyes were holding Trent's attention. "Well, if there's more to this, why don't you tell me what it is?" he said.

So Trent told him about the bragging Robbie had been doing and how Robbie had overheard Trent and Wilson making fun of him.

"So, I guess he was pretty mad about that," his dad said.

"Sure he was. But all we were doing was messing around. And you can't believe how stupid he's been acting lately."

"It sounds like you think Robbie is the one with the problem."

"Well, yeah. He's the one who started all the bragging. Him and Gloria."

"And you didn't do anything wrong?"

"Both of us acted pretty stupid, I guess. And the trouble is, the whole team is messed up because of it."

"So what are you going to do about it?"

"I don't know. What do you think I should do?"

Mr. Lubak sat up straight, crossed his arms, and thought for a time. "Well, first off, I'm glad you're admitting your share of the fault. That's very mature."

Trent smiled a little. "When a guy throws a ball, and it doesn't even come down in the same baseball park, it's not hard to see that he can make a mistake."

His dad laughed. "That was *some* throw," he said. "You'll never forget that one."

"You still haven't told me what to do."

"You've got a practice in the morning, don't you?"

"Yeah."

"Well, that'll be your chance. I'd let the whole thing cool off overnight, and then see what you can do tomorrow."

"Are you saying I should tell Robbie I'm sorry?"

"I don't know. Maybe you do have some things you're sorry about. And maybe you *should* say that. But the one thing I'm sure of is this: Until you and Robbie work things out, the team is never going to get together."

Yeah. That much was very clear to Trent. But Robbie was angrier than ever now—and Trent wasn't sure how to get around that.

All that evening and early the next morning—when Trent woke up much sooner than he had intended to—he thought about what he could say. On his way to the field, he ran through different ways to get the conversation started. But no matter what he came up with, he always imagined Robbie yelling at him.

When Trent reached the park, a couple of

the Scrappers were already on the infield: Wilson and, of all people, Gloria. They were playing catch.

"Hey," Wilson said. Something in his little grin seemed to say, "I'm not mad at Gloria anymore."

But Gloria took a more direct approach. "Hey, Lubak, it's over. Okay?"

"What?"

"Me and Wilson talked it out. I told him I like to talk smack because it makes the game more fun. And the only reason I say I'm good is because that makes me try to be as good as I say I am. That's just the way I am, and all you wimpy boys don't need to get your sweet little feelings hurt."

Wilson grinned again. "I told her, 'Say what you want. I won't listen.'"

Trent shrugged. "Fair enough," he said. But he still didn't like it. Gloria could destroy a guy like Martin, the way she sometimes worked him over. Talking to the other team was one thing, but Gloria also chewed on her own teammates.

But it was time to patch things up, and if Wilson and Gloria were okay with what Gloria was doing, Trent wasn't going to get another argument going.

"We'll beat those jerks the next time we play them," Gloria said, and suddenly she tossed the ball to Trent, who hadn't even put on his glove yet.

He caught the ball bare-handed, chucked it back, and said, "It didn't matter whether I threw home or threw to Robbie. I was already too late by then. Where I messed up was when I—"

"You took the wrong angle to the ball. You're slower than ketchup from a bottle, Trent. You ought to know that by now."

"Yeah. That's what I was going to say. Sort of."

"Okay . . . well . . . don't do it again. Don't be so stupid."

"All right."

Gloria put her hands on her hips and glared at Trent. "Oh, brother. I can't take guys like you. Tell me to shut my mouth and we'll get along a lot better."

"Okay. Shut your mouth."

"Shut your own mouth or I'll tear your lips off." She laughed.

Trent laughed, too, but he wasn't sure that Gloria's way of solving the problem was going to work.

More players started showing up, and then Coach Carlton pulled up in his old pickup and walked over to the diamond. "Hello, Trent," he said. "How do you feel? Better?"

"Yes and no."

"What do you mean?"

"I'm not mad at anyone now, but I still feel pretty rotten."

"What do you feel rotten about?"

"About messing up the play—and letting the run score."

"Well, that's something you can learn from. It's that fight you and Robbie got into that I don't understand."

"I'm going to work that out," Trent said.

"Good. I told Robbie that the two of you needed to have a talk. I know he jumped on you about that throw—and I told him that wasn't right. He said he knew that, but then he said you had done something to him. I didn't want to hear any more about it. I just told him to call you and talk. Did he do that?"

"Not yet."

"Well, all right. Today is the day. I'm count-ing on both of you."

But Robbie didn't arrive until the last sec-ond, and when he did, he avoided Trent. He walked over to Martin and Chad, two guys he almost never spent much time with. He said something, and all three of them started to laugh.

Trent didn't know what that was about, but he had a feeling it wasn't a good sign.

Thurlow and his mother were the last to arrive—about five minutes late—and when they did, Coach Carlton called the team together.

He stuck his hands deep in his pants pockets—those same old reddish-colored pants he always wore—and looked down at everybody. "That was a tough one yesterday. You played good ball—or at least you did for five innings. And then you quit. You know that as well as I do, and I'm not going to make a big speech about it. All I've got to say is, it's now or never."

He waited. Trent wasn't exactly sure what the coach meant, but he had pretty good idea.

"I told you at the start of the season that I didn't want to coach a bunch of kids who wouldn't support one another. You seem to make a little headway, and then we have another one of these flare-ups. But I've seen enough of that. We're not going to have any more. The next time it happens, we start kicking people off the team. Either that, or you look for a new coach."

Again, he looked around, waited.

"Understood?"

"Yeah," everyone said.

"Okay. Those involved in yesterday's squabble have promised to work it out. For now, let's get serious about some hard practice."

The kids got up and headed to their positions. Practice went well, too.

The coach worked first on throwing to the cutoff man. And he made a good point—one Trent hadn't really thought about: "The reason to throw to the cutoff is not just that a long throw can go wrong. It's also that a lot can change while the ball is in the air. A runner can take a base standing up while the ball travels the entire length of the field. Short throws give us better control of the game. Baseball is the only game where the defense controls the ball."

Then he looked right at Robbie. "On the

other hand, when a guy is rounding third, and there are no other runners, sometimes you have to throw to the plate—if you have the arm to get the ball there."

Trent saw Robbie nod, but he knew what Robbie was thinking: Trent *didn't* have the arm for that.

The players paid attention, and they worked hard. Trent wasn't sure that feelings on the team were any better, but at least no one was saying anything negative.

All during practice Trent waited for Robbie to speak to him, but he never did. And then when the coach ended the practice, Robbie headed straight to his bike. Trent followed. As the coach had said, it was now or never.

"Robbie, can I talk to you?" Trent said as he walked up to him.

"Sure." Robbie turned around, but Trent couldn't read what he was thinking. There was no sign of friendship in his face.

"The coach told us both to talk to each other, the way I heard it."

"Yep. That's what he told me anyway."

"But you were leaving."

"He didn't say when."

Trent took a deep breath. This wasn't going to be easy. "Look, I know you're mad about Wilson and me making fun of you. I'm sorry we—"

"Wouldn't you be mad?"

"Yeah. I would. But we started to fool around and got carried away. We didn't mean it as bad as you took it."

Robbie turned toward his bike. He began to move the dials on his combination lock. "Here's what makes me mad," he said. "We've been friends almost forever. Or at least that's what I *thought*. I don't think I'd do something like that to you."

"I know. You probably wouldn't. I'm sorry." He stuck his glove under his arm. "I should have come and talked to you earlier."

Robbie looked back at him and nodded. That seemed to be an acceptance of the apology. He finished getting his bike free from the rack and pulled it out. He didn't look at Trent when he said, "I shouldn't have said anything about that throw you made. I was just mad."

"Okay. Let's just drop this whole thing—and bring the team together."

Again, Robbie nodded. But then he said, "You just said that you should have come and talked to me earlier. If you had, what would you have said? I need to know."

"I just felt like you had started bragging and talking big. Like Gloria. I don't like that kind of stuff."

"And that's all you wanted to say?"

"Yeah."

"So you wouldn't have said you were jealous because I'm playing better than you are?"

Trent was surprised. "No," he said. "You're better than me. But I'm not jealous about it."

"So that was it, huh? You were going to talk to me, but you weren't going to tell the truth?"

Trent didn't want to get in another fight, but he was getting angrier by the second. "If that's what you want to think, go ahead and think it," he finally said.

"That *is* what I think," Robbie said. Then he threw his leg over his bike, got on, and rode away.

CHAPTER SEVEN

After Robbie rode off, Wilson walked over to Trent. "Did you guys get things worked out?" he asked.

"No. He's still mad."

"I don't believe it. When is the guy going to let loose of this thing?"

Trent didn't answer. He was wondering the same thing. But he was also thinking about Robbie's accusation.

"Do you want to go over to the pitching machines and hit some balls?" Wilson asked.

"I don't have any money."

"I've got a little. I'll split it with you. At least we can each get a few swings in. Right now I think we've got the two worst batting averages on the team."

That wasn't exactly true. For one thing,

Wilson was hitting better than Trent. And the subs, along with Ollie, were hitting worse than either one of them. But Trent was close to the bottom, and he knew it. So he got on his bike and rode with Wilson to the batting cages. But his heart wasn't in it.

"Wilson, are you jealous of Robbie and Thurlow?" he asked, as they pumped their bikes down the street, side by side.

"Sure."

"You are?"

"Hey, I'd give anything to be like Thurlow. Fast and powerful at the same time. The guy is amazing."

"What about his attitude? You wouldn't want that, would you?"

"He's kind of messed up right now. But he never used to have a bad attitude. He's going to get over that, and then he's going to be great. Really great."

"And that doesn't bother you?"

"No. Why should it?"

That's where Trent had to stop. He knew it *did* bother him that he wasn't as good as Thurlow or Robbie. Sometimes he even caught himself hoping that Robbie would strike out or make an error.

Trent wanted the team to win, but he got tired of Robbie being the star all the time. It didn't seem fair. Trent worked just as hard as Robbie, probably harder, and he cared as much about baseball. So why wasn't he as good?

When they were younger, Robbie and Trent had talked about making it to the majors. It seemed like maybe both could do it, too. Now it looked like Robbie had a much better chance. Maybe Trent couldn't blame Robbie for that— but that didn't mean he had to like it.

But all that stuff sort of worried Trent. He didn't like the way he felt about himself when he admitted that maybe Robbie was right about him.

It was just past noon when Trent and Wilson pulled up at the batting cages and locked their bikes. It was starting to get really hot, but at least a little breeze was blowing.

The two boys stood in neighboring cages for half an hour or so, letting the sweat roll off them as they swung at the balls being fired from the pitching machines.

When Trent glanced over at Wilson from

time to time, he was looking pretty good. But Trent couldn't seem to concentrate. He wasn't hitting the ball at all well.

By the time the boys left the cages, Trent had another question for Wilson. "Were we mad at Robbie and Gloria because they were bragging—or did it just bother us that they're so good?"

"I don't know about you, but I was just sick of all their talk. I *want* them to play well."

Trent nodded. He had thought all along that that's what he wanted, too. Now he wondered.

"Hey, look." Wilson pointed toward one of the cages down the line.

It took a moment for Trent to realize what Wilson was pointing at. Then he recognized Thurlow standing at the plate. He looked focused, too. Trent and Wilson watched as he cracked several pitches, driving line shots. The machine was set high, really humming, but Thurlow hit everything that came at him.

"Wow," Wilson whispered when Thurlow's machine turned off. "Now *that* is what I wish I could do."

"Why is he practicing?" Trent asked.

"I don't know. Maybe he cares more than he lets on."

Thurlow walked toward the control box to drop in some more quarters. That's when he looked up and saw Trent and Wilson watching him.

Thurlow looked surprised for a moment, but then he smiled, as if to say, "Okay, so you caught me."

Trent and Wilson walked over to Thurlow's cage. "What's up?" Wilson asked.

"Nothin'."

"Do you come over here very often?"

"I don't know. Once in a while."

"I thought you didn't like baseball."

Thurlow looked away. He said, rather quietly, "I like baseball all right. I just don't want anybody to tell me that I have to play."

Trent smiled. "Man, if I could play the way you do, I'd want to do nothing else."

Thurlow looked at him curiously for a time. Finally, he said, "That's no reason to play."

"What do you mean?"

"You don't play *because* you're good. You play

because you want to get better. I'm thinking more about basketball these days."

"Then why are you here?"

"Just something to do."

"I don't believe that, Thurlow," Wilson said. "I think you love the feel of hitting that ball. You're a baseball player, whether you admit it or not."

Thurlow shrugged. He had some quarters in his hand. He was about to start sliding them into the machine when he looked up at Wilson. "Sometimes I start thinking I don't mind playing with this team. And then everybody starts *talking*, and I get sick of the whole thing again."

"We've got some great players, we just—"

"You don't have to have great players. You need people who know what they can do and do it. On this team, everybody wants to be the big shot."

He dropped the quarters in the machine and went back to whacking line drives.

But all the rest of the day Trent thought about the things Thurlow had said. And he talked again with his dad. "Thurlow's right," Mr. Lubak told Trent. "Sometimes the teams with a lot of great players fall apart. Everyone wants to get his own stats and be the star. A good team has role players—people who are willing to put down a bunt or hit the ball behind a runner, to move him over. Then someone else drives the runs in."

All week Trent kept running that idea through his head, and he felt like he was starting to understand himself better than he ever had before.

What he wanted to do was call Robbie, say, "Let's forget all this stuff," and then hang out with him the way they used to. But Robbie didn't call, and Trent decided he had some things he needed to *show* Robbie, not *tell* him.

The team had a pretty good practice on Thursday. But Robbie didn't have much to say to Trent, and no one had much to say about the upcoming game. The Scrappers were playing the Stingrays again. That meant facing "Bullet" Bennett. They had beaten him before, but they had gotten some lucky breaks.

On the day of the game, Trent was more nervous than usual. There were things he felt he had to handle right this time. When he got out of the car, before the game, he barely heard his parents wish him well. He nodded and walked toward the dugout, where the Scrappers were gathering.

Trent sensed something strange in the players. There was no quarreling, no bad feelings that Trent could pick up on, but there was also no excitement. He suspected that the team was ready to mail this one in.

The Scrappers had come so close to beating the Mustangs, and yet they had lost. Now there was nothing to get psyched about. The team had no chance to win the first-half championship. The Mustangs had that for sure.

Still, Trent knew the Scrappers needed to get some momentum going. Then, maybe they could win the second half, and even the league championship in a play-off. But he wasn't sure anyone else still believed that could happen—or cared.

The coach gave his usual little pep talk, but no one seemed to be paying much attention. Everyone got up and shouted, "Let's go get 'em!"—or whatever—but there was no spirit behind it.

What Trent knew was that the kids on the team weren't so divided now, but they weren't united either. He also knew it was going to take some action, not words, to make things change.

In the first inning Bullet did his thing. The Scrappers all said they weren't afraid of him this time, but they sat on the bench and watched—almost silent. His fastball was thumping the catcher's mitt like a blow from a sledgehammer. And when he went to his curve, the thing was unhittable.

Someone in the Stingrays' bleachers kept yelling, "Hey Scrappers, you're in trouble today. Bullet's got his stuff."

Jack Gibbs, Gloria's dad—with a mouth like his daughter's—yelled back, "The harder he throws the ball, the farther we hit it."

But Trent didn't see any sign that the Scrappers believed that.

The good news was, Ollie was in a nice groove, too. He didn't have quite the pop in his fastball that Bullet did, but he was changing speeds, mixing his pitches—and, above all, throwing strikes. Whatever Ollie was saying to himself today was working.

The Scrappers played some solid defense, too. Adam did drop a ball at first, for an error. But he made a big stretch a few minutes later and dug one out of the dirt. Jeremy also made a nice catch on a little fly ball that easily could have dropped in front of him.

So nothing was going wrong. But there was no electricity out there, and it was going to take something extra to have a chance against Bullet.

When Trent came up to bat in the third inning, the game was still scoreless, and the Scrappers had only one out. He really wanted to do something to get the team going. He was batting eighth today, with Ollie in the ninth spot. If Trent and Ollie could get something started, the top of the order would come up with a chance to do some damage.

Trent took a fastball outside for a ball. Then he let a curve go by even though it broke over the plate for a strike.

Trent was almost sure that Bennett would come back with his hard stuff, and he had his doubts whether he could hit it. So he tried something different. He squared off, got the bat out, and laid down a bunt.

It wasn't perfect. The ball rolled a little too far up the third base line. But the pitcher and the third baseman weren't expecting it. Trent strained for every bit of speed he could find in himself, but he saw the third baseman charging hard.

The play was close, but Trent hit the bag an instant before the throw came in, and the ump called him safe. He heard the reaction from his teammates immediately. "All right. Now we've got something started," Tracy yelled.

But Bullet overpowered Ollie. He took two pitches for strikes and then swung weakly on an evil-looking curveball.

With two outs, Wanda told Trent, "Be ready to run on anything."

So when Jeremy poked at a fastball, Trent got a good jump. The ball looped just over the second baseman's head. Trent looked to Coach Carlton, saw him wave his arm, and pushed hard to make it to third.

That's when the Stingrays started making mistakes. The right fielder tried to throw all the way to third to get Trent. The throw was late, and Jeremy used the chance to take second.

That brought Robbie up.

"Okay, Robbie, bring us home," Trent yelled. "You can hit this guy."

Trent and Jeremy had made something happen. Now Robbie was the guy who had a chance to time Bullet's fastball and get the team in front.

Trent felt good about that. He *wanted* Robbie to get a hit. He had used his own ability to do what he could do, and now he wanted his buddy to do his part.

Robbie glanced down to third base, nodded to Trent, and then stepped to the plate. The first pitch was a killer fastball at the knees. Robbie started to swing and then held up. The ump called it a ball.

The next pitch was up a little. Robbie played it smart again. He took it for ball two.

With first base open, Bennett could afford to walk Robbie. But if he did, that would only mean he would have to face Gloria. And that was no easier.

Maybe that's why Bullet took something off his fastball. He chucked it down the middle. And Robbie *crushed* it.

He hit a line drive that got past the left fielder before he could react.

Robbie held up with a double—the coach signaling him to play it safe—but he might well have gone for three.

Now Gloria was up, and Robbie wasn't giving her a hard time. "Bring me home," he was telling her. "Let's keep it going."

But she wasn't talking. She was concentrating, looking determined.

As it turned out, she got under a pitch and lifted the ball high in the air to center. The center fielder made the catch and the inning was over.

The Scrappers had only gotten off to a two-run lead, but that wasn't bad. At least some good things were happening now.

And Trent could feel the team coming to life.

CHAPTER EIGHT

Trent took his position in left field. He rocked from side to side a little to keep his legs loose. He couldn't remember who was up next, but when he saw it was "Petey" Peterson, the little redheaded shortstop, he moved up a little, along with Jeremy and Thurlow.

Petey was so short he didn't have much of a strike zone. Ollie missed high with his first two throws. But Petey didn't like to walk. He swung hard at the next pitch. From left field Trent heard the ping of the bat a split second after contact. Then he saw the ball bounce toward Robbie, at third.

The ball was hit fairly hard, but Robbie stepped up to meet it.

The ball looked like a routine grounder. Still,

Trent ran toward the line to back up Robbie, just in case something went wrong.

Suddenly the ball—for no reason Trent could see—took a high hop. Trent was sure the ball was heading over Robbie's head.

But Robbie came out of his crouch and leaped high. He snagged the ball with his glove hand and already had it in his bare hand when he hit the ground.

Petey was fast. But Robbie didn't panic. He got his balance, planted his back foot, and rifled the ball.

Trent had slowed to a stop, and now he watched the throw. He held his breath until he saw the ump's arm jerk into the air. "Yes!" he shouted, and Robbie's head swung around.

"You da man, Robbie," Trent said.

Robbie looked a little surprised. But then he said, "You got us started. *You* da man."

Both boys laughed. And Trent liked the feeling.

"No way. *I'm* the man! Or the closest thing to one," Gloria yelled. Now all three were laughing.

Trent turned and trotted back to left field.

He felt like a big weight had been lifted off his shoulders.

The next batter was a girl named Elise Harris. She was a solid hitter, with good bat control. She managed to foul off five or six tough pitches before she worked her way to a walk.

But Ollie didn't seem to let that bother him. He fired two blistering fastballs at the next man up. The batter—the Stingrays' center fielder— was quickly in the hole, 0 and 2.

Ollie then moved the ball outside, and the batter didn't chase it. But when he came with a change-up, the guy mistimed his swing. He popped the ball up, and Adam drifted into foul territory to take it for out number two.

The big catcher, Elvin Badger, was up after that. But Ollie was in control. He set him up with some good fastballs, then struck the guy out on an off-speed curve.

Trent knew that if Ollie kept pitching like that, two runs might be enough today. But he also knew that Ollie usually had his troubles sooner or later. The Scrappers definitely needed more runs.

In the dugout all the Scrappers were telling

Ollie to keep it up. And some of them told Robbie he had made a great play. Robbie kept saying, "Thanks," but that was all.

Gloria told him, "I would have made that play. I just would have made it look easy—and no one would have said much about it."

Robbie smiled and sat down on the bench. He didn't say a word to Gloria. But he also didn't walk over and sit next to Trent, as Trent had hoped he would.

The trouble between Trent and Robbie seemed to have eased up, but Trent wondered whether they would ever be close friends again.

"That was a great play Robbie made," Trent told Wilson.

Wilson nodded. "That's a reaction play. Some people can do it and some can't, but there's no way to teach something like that."

"Robbie has good instincts, doesn't he?"

"Yep. He does. But the play you made—seeing the third baseman playing back and putting down a bunt. That's a smart play. That's something not everybody does—play and think at the same time."

"Guys like Robbie—and Thurlow—they

don't have to think. They just do the right thing."

"Well, not exactly. They have to think, too. But they don't have to think up ways to get on base. They can just swing away and figure something good will happen."

"I wish I could do that."

"Hey, some guys are naturals. And some have to work at it. But both kinds can get the job done. Maybe guys like you and me don't have as much talent, but if we play hard—and smart— we can still help the team."

That fit in with what Trent had been telling himself all week. He wished he had Robbie's talent, but he couldn't do anything about that. What he could do was get the most out of the talent he did have.

The Scrappers didn't score in the fourth or fifth innings. And finally, in the bottom of the fifth, the Stingrays came to life.

Ollie didn't pitch all that badly, and the Scrappers' defense didn't mess up, but the Stingrays showed they had some good hitters. They put together three singles that produced one run. But with two outs, the Scrappers still had a chance to escape with only minor damage. That's when big Elvin came up to bat again, with two men on base.

Ollie kept the first two pitches outside, obviously trying to get the big guy to chase a bad one. But Elvin didn't swing. And then Ollie grooved a pitch and Elvin *thumped* it.

The ball took off like an easy fly. But it just kept carrying. Trent ran to the fence, waited, thought he might have a chance—but it cleared the fence by twenty feet. Home run.

The Scrappers had suddenly gone from two up to two down, 4 to 2.

Trent walked back to his position. He watched the Stingrays celebrate, and he looked around at his own teammates. He was afraid they might roll over and play dead after something like that.

But that's not what he saw. The Scrappers were pounding their gloves and shouting back and forth to one another. "We're all right," Coach Carlton was yelling. "We'll get those runs back." The players were saying the same thing.

When Ollie got the final out, and the Scrappers ran to the dugout, all the players were showing how much they wanted this game now. "Let's go, Wilson," Jeremy yelled as the big guy walked to the plate.

All of Wilson's work at the batting cages seemed to pay off, too. He slammed a Bennett fastball *hard*. It sailed high and long, over the center fielder's head. It didn't clear the fence on the fly, but it bounced over for a ground-rule double.

That brought up Thurlow. As Thurlow put one foot into the batter's box and adjusted his helmet, he looked toward second base. Trent saw him nod to Wilson, as if to say, "You did your part, now I'll do mine."

Thurlow looked the way he had at the batting cages: set, ready, serious. For some reason, he had decided to try today.

Trent could never figure out when Thurlow was going to come to a game prepared to play. Maybe Thurlow didn't know himself. As much as anything, he seemed to like a challenge, and Bullet Bennett certainly offered that.

Thurlow stared at Bullet and waited. And Bullet took his time. The guy was nervous.

The pitch was a firecracker, but it was out

over the plate. Thurlow uncoiled like a spring. His hands flashed, and he caught the ball *full* on the sweet part of the bat.

The ball shot over the left field fence so fast that Bullet hardly had time to turn around and see it disappear.

The score was tied, 4 to 4.

The Scrappers all jumped to their feet and screamed as they watched Wilson and Thurlow trot around the bases. "They're like Mantle and Maris," Trent heard Robbie say. "How would you like to be a pitcher and have to face those two?"

Trent felt a little funny about that. Wilson was powerful, but he hadn't been hitting very well lately. Was it going to turn out that *everyone* on the team was better than he was?

But he heard his parents cheering for Wilson and Thurlow, and he knew what he had to do. He tried to yell louder than anyone, and then he went out and greeted them both as they crossed home plate.

When everyone came back to the dugout, Gloria was pacing up and down. Trent could see how much she wanted to win this game. Somehow, she had gotten dirt all over her uniform. She looked like she had been in a fight—and was ready for another one.

"You think it's tough to face Wilson and Thurlow?" she barked. "Just think of facing Robbie and me right before those guys come up."

Trent had to admit it was true. It was a murderer's row, and with a leadoff batter like Jeremy, the heart of the Scrappers' batting order was *tough*. The problem was, the rest of the order was not nearly so scary—and Trent was part of the problem. Those were the players who had to come through if this team was ever going to be really good.

But Trent was starting to have some faith in this team. He knew darn well the Scrappers could beat anyone in the league when they played their best.

"You know what, Scrappers?" he yelled. "We're getting to be *good*. Did you ever think that would happen?"

"I knew *I* would be," Gloria responded. "I wondered about the rest of you guys."

Everyone laughed. Tracy was outside the

dugout, getting ready to head to the plate. "You always know how to say just the right thing, Gloria," she said, but she was laughing, and that seemed another good sign.

Tracy marched to the plate. And she used her head, as usual. Bullet was obviously losing some confidence, and his pitches were all over the place. Tracy watched the pitches closely, took anything that wasn't over the plate, and ended up with a walk.

Adam followed Tracy, and he hit a long fly ball for an out, but Tracy tagged up and moved to second.

With one out and the go-ahead run on second, Trent was up again.

And he was scared.

He didn't want to let the team down now. His faith in the Scrappers was growing. His doubts were about himself.

But Trent remembered what the coach always said. In a situation like this, it was good to hit behind the runner. If Trent couldn't drive Tracy home, he should at least open the way for her to make it to third on an out.

The first pitch was a curveball that started

over the plate but broke outside. The guy was still fighting his control, and Trent had to take advantage of that.

The next pitch was a fastball, but it wasn't the high-speed stuff that Bennett usually threw. Trent waited on the pitch and poked it to the right side. He hit it solid, too, and it darted past the second baseman and into right field.

Tracy had to wait for a second to see the ball get through, but then she took off hard. Trent looked around to see the coach's arm swinging in a big circle.

Tracy cruised around third and raced toward the plate.

The Stingrays' right fielder made a smart play this time. He hit the second baseman—the cutoff—with a good throw. She spun around, saw she had no chance to get Tracy at the plate, and faked a throw to first, chasing Trent back to the bag.

"That's it, Trent. Way to go!" Gloria was screaming. Robbie and all the rest were cheering, too. Trent loved the feeling.

Now the Stingrays' coach was walking to the mound. As Trent waited at first, he looked at the bleachers and spotted his parents. They were waving and cheering, too. He knew he was smiling, but he tried not to act as excited as he was.

The coach talked to Bullet for a minute or so. Then he walked back to the dugout without making a pitching change.

Bennett toed the rubber and checked Trent at first. Then he threw a fastball at the knees, which Ollie took for a strike. Trent clapped his hands and yelled, "Keep the heat on, Ollie. Let's get some more runs."

Bennett went to his curve, but it didn't break much, and Ollie was all over it. He drove the ball all the way to the right field corner.

As the right fielder chased down the ball, Trent and Ollie—the two slowest runners on the team—ran as hard as they could. And they bulled their way around the diamond.

Trent rounded third and headed for home. But out of the corner of his eye, he saw the relay throw darting toward the plate. "Get down! Slide!" Coach Carlton yelled, as he ran down the line alongside Trent.

Trent had worked hard on his slide. He kept pushing hard until the last second, and then he dropped down with one leg stretching toward the plate and the other tucked under him.

Dirt flew, and he felt Elvin's big glove slam against his ankle. For a moment, he wasn't sure.

But then he heard, "Safe!"

Trent jumped straight in the air. Then he ran to the dugout as his teammates came out to welcome him.

"We need more runs!" everyone was shouting. "Come on, Jeremy. Bring Ollie home."
But Jeremy got under a ball and popped it up. The catcher moved over and made the catch. Robbie dug in and got ready. On the first pitch, he knocked a fly into center field. It seemed to have a chance to get into the left center gap, but the center fielder made a good run and hauled it in.

The inning was over, but at least the Scrappers had a two-run lead, and the bottom of the order had come through.

Trent grabbed his glove and ran from the dugout, but as he reached the third base line, Coach Carlton was waiting for him. "Come here a sec, Trent," he said.

Trent had been about to run on past, but he held up.

"Let me ask you something," the coach said.

"Sure."

"Did you try to hit the ball to the right side—on purpose?"

"Well, yeah. I thought we were always supposed to do that. Isn't that the best way to move a runner ahead?"

"Yes, it is. But it isn't something most kids can do. They don't have that much bat control."

"Well, Bullet doesn't have his best stuff right now. If he had—"

"Trent, listen to me. Don't sell yourself short. You're a solid player. You know the game. You get the most out of your ability. If every player out here did what you do, no one would ever beat us."

"Thanks, Coach."

Trent didn't run back to the field. He floated. And when he ran past third base, Robbie said, "Way to come through for us, Trent." That was even better.

But when Trent reached the field and settled

down, he also faced reality: the Scrappers had only a two-run lead. The team really needed a win today, not another blown lead and another loss. Everyone had to keep pulling together and put this one away.

CHAPTER NINE

Ollie put the Stingrays away—one-two-three—in bottom of the sixth, but the Scrappers' "murderer's row" didn't scare anyone in the top of the seventh. So it all came down to the bottom of the seventh. The lead was still 6 to 4.

Once Ollie finished his warm-up pitches, Wilson stepped out in front of the plate and shouted, "All right. No letdown. Let's keep our heads in this game."

Trent wondered whether Wilson was thinking of that terrible throw Trent had made in the last game. And Robbie seemed to read Trent's mind. He turned around. "We're going to get these guys today," he yelled.

Robbie had certainly meant "the whole team" when he said "we." But Trent thought he also meant "the two of us." That's how he chose to take it anyway. He waved to Robbie and shouted, "That's right. Let's do it."

This was how baseball was supposed to be. He loved the feeling on the team right now.

"Three more outs," everyone was yelling. And they sounded sure of themselves.

But some of that confidence quickly disappeared. The first batter timed one of Ollie's fastballs and drove it straight over Gloria's head.

Trent charged the ball, picked it up on a high bounce, and then fired to Cindy at second, who was in the game for Tracy. The runner held at first.

"That's all right," Gloria was yelling. "Take the easy one at second."

But one of the Stingrays' subs—not much of a hitter—also punched one of Ollie's fastballs through the infield for another single. Thurlow cut it off quickly, but now there were runners on first and second, with no outs. Trent felt his stomach start to churn.

"Here we go again," Trent mumbled to himself. As he watched, he saw what he feared. Ollie was pressing and couldn't find the strike zone.

He walked the next batter, and the bases were loaded.

The Stingrays and all their fans were going crazy. Ollie turned around and ducked his head, as though he had already lost the game. Trent just couldn't believe that everything had turned around this fast.

Coach Carlton yelled, "Time-out," and walked to the mound.

As Trent watched from the outfield, he wasn't surprised to see the coach pat Ollie on the shoulder and take the ball from him. What did surprise him was that Ollie was heading for right field, not first base.

Trent suddenly realized what was happening. The coach was going to put Thurlow on the mound.

Thurlow in to *pitch*? What was the coach thinking? There was no question that Thurlow had a powerful arm, but as far as Trent knew the guy had never pitched in his life.

But Thurlow trotted to the mound, talked to the coach for a few seconds, and then gave a nod. The coach gave him the ball and walked away.

When Thurlow began to take his warm-up pitches, Trent jogged toward the infield. Gloria and Robbie were standing together. "What's going on?" Trent called to them.

They both turned around, and Robbie said, "The coach said, 'Have you ever pitched before?' And Thurlow said, 'Yeah. A little.' So Coach said, 'Take over. Throw strikes.' Then he said something about all the Stingrays being afraid of Thurlow. That part did make some sense."

"Hey, I think it's the smartest move he could have made," Gloria said. "Thurlow's got the best arm on the team—and when you challenge the guy, he comes through."

Trent nodded and jogged back to left field. And he hoped for the best. But he kept thinking about the bases loaded with no outs—and the Scrappers only up by two.

But Trent could see that something *was* happening to the Stingrays. The three guys on base were looking around like they didn't know their jobs anymore. In the dugout the players were all huddled up, trying to figure this out. Even their coach looked confused. Everybody seemed to know that Thurlow was not a pitcher—not normally.

Thurlow's first couple of warm-up pitches looked like batting-practice throws—as though he were trying to find the range. But now he was rearing back and throwing *hard*. Dust flew from Wilson's mitt each time a pitch pounded into it.

But the ball was sailing all over the place! A couple of the pitches, Wilson couldn't even catch.

When the ump called for a final throw, Thurlow let loose with a rocket that flew way over Wilson's head. When it hit the padded part of the backstop, it made a sound like a hand grenade and left a bright white mark on the royal blue lining.

The Stingrays in the dugout were all standing up, watching, but they were silent as statues. No one had a word to yell at Thurlow.

When the ump called for a batter, Wilson ran halfway to the mound and then shouted in a voice that everyone could hear, "Try not to throw inside. You could hurt someone."

Petey walked to the plate.

Almost.

He stayed well back in the batter's box.

The first pitch was another bomb, but high, right at eye level. It was nowhere near Petey, but he bailed out of the box like a guy ducking from gunfire.

Slowly, he set up again and looked out at Thurlow.

The next pitch was a good fastball, though not as hard, and it must have nicked the outside edge of the strike zone. Petey was leaning away. One and one.

The next pitch was right down the tube, and fast. Petey was still leaning away, but he tried to take a swipe at the ball. One and two.

And then Thurlow fired another missile, right over the plate. Petey tried to swing and jump backward at the same time.

Strike three!

One away. The Scrappers went crazy. Everyone was screaming for Thurlow. Robbie turned around and yelled to Trent, "Shift a little toward center. No one is going to get around on Thurlow."

Robbie was laughing, but Trent knew he was right. He moved in a little and shifted over. He waved Jeremy toward right field.

The Stingrays' coach called a time-out and walked over to his dugout. None of the Scrappers could hear what he was saying, but the next batter—Elise—came up and took her normal stance in the box, not giving ground the way Petey had.

The first pitch was at her knees. She jerked her legs back so fast, she threw herself off balance. She almost fell down.

"Come on, ump," the Stingrays' coach was yelling from his box at third base. "He's trying to hit my players."

"Not even close, Coach," the umpire shouted back at him. "That pitch barely missed the inside corner of the plate."

But Elise stayed in the box better than Petey had. She didn't swing, but she waited Thurlow out, and she worked the count full.

Another ball and the Stingrays would get a one-run gift.

But Thurlow got the ball over the plate with plenty on it. Elise took a good swing—and missed.

Two away.

The Scrappers could win this game after all. Trent felt new life pumping back into his veins.

When the next batter started toward the plate, Wilson called time-out and ran to the mound. Trent could see Thurlow and Wilson laughing as they talked back and forth.

But Trent knew that the next batter was a much better hitter than the last two. He was a kid named Reynolds who had played on the league's all-star team the year before. He wasn't going to be scared so easily.

The first pitch looked like it might be low—from Trent's point of view. But the umpire called it a strike.

The next pitch was up a little more, and Reynolds went after it. He swung a little late, but he got a piece of it and fouled it off. Trent shifted even more toward center field.

Reynolds stepped out of the box, gripped the bat tightly, and pounded it on the ground. He was clearly trying to psych himself up to get back in there and do something with all those runners on base.

This pitch could end the game.

Reynolds started to swing and laid off. The ump called the pitch a ball, even though it looked like strike three from the outfield.

Trent's mouth was so dry he couldn't have spit if he had to.

Another pitch. Another close one. But the ump called it ball two.

A walk could put the tying run at third base. Even more, it might break Thurlow's confidence. Thurlow wasn't used to being out there on the mound in a situation like this.

When Thurlow got the return throw this time, he bent over and glared at the batter. But Reynolds stared right back at him.

Wilson set the target at Reynolds's knees. And this time Thurlow seemed to hit that target. But Reynolds let the pitch go, and the ump called it a ball. The count was full.

The Stingrays had found their voices again. They were yelling at Thurlow, yelling to Reynolds. And the crowd was really into it, the fans for both teams putting up a roar.

Thurlow took his time, but Trent liked what he saw. The guy was into this—part of the team. He put his foot on the rubber, looked for the sign, which was kind of a joke. He was only throwing heat, and everyone knew it.

All the runners led off, and Trent felt his whole body go on alert.

This was it!

Thurlow cut loose with another firecracker, but Reynolds was ready—and finally had the timing right.

He laced the pitch hard, past Gloria and into left center. Trent had shifted enough that he was in a good spot to cut the ball off, but there was no chance to catch it on the fly. He ran hard, got to as quickly as he could, and then spun around. He squared up and set his feet. Runners were on the move, all around the bases. He wasn't sure what to do.

Gloria set up for the cutoff throw. But Trent also saw Wilson, ready to take the throw at home. There was no chance to get the first runner, but Trent wanted to cut down the guy from second at the plate—and keep the tying run from scoring.

His first thought was to cut loose with the ball, try to throw all the way to Wilson, on the fly. But he knew what he had been taught. He stepped into his throw and launched the ball right at Gloria's head—low and hard. Wilson would tell her whether to cut the throw or let it through.

The ball sailed like a lance, right on target. The Stingrays' coach saw that and yelled, "Hold up. Hold up."

The runner had rounded third, but now he put on the brakes.

"Cut it!" Wilson bellowed.

Gloria reached up, took the throw, and turned toward the runner. He was caught in no-man's-land, halfway home.

Then Gloria did exactly what the coach always said to do. She ran straight at the runner and forced him to decide which way he was going to go.

The runner suddenly bolted toward third, and Gloria fired to Robbie. He put the tag down as the runner dove headfirst at the bag.

"*Out!*" the umpire yelled.

It took Trent about two full seconds to realize that the game was over. When he did, he jumped straight in the air. By the time he landed, he was already in motion. He dashed toward Robbie, who was running toward him.

"Great throw!" Robbie was yelling.

"Great play at third!"

The two leaped into the air and banged their chests, landed on their feet, and then grabbed each other by the shoulders.

"You da man!" Robbie yelled.

"No, you da man!"

"No, you da man!"

"I keep telling you, *I'm* the man," Gloria was yelling into their faces, but she was patting both of their backs.

Most of the team had collected together around Thurlow. He was walking off the field, trying to get away, but the mob was moving with him. Trent and Robbie and Gloria all joined them.

Wilson laughed when he saw them. "I told Thurlow to throw his last warm-up pitch all the way to the backstop. We had those guys shaking in their boots."

Trent liked that. He slapped hands with Wilson, and then he worked his way through the crowd to Thurlow. "Way to go. I didn't know you could pitch," he said.

Robbie reached out and slapped hands with Thurlow, too. "Way to come through," he said.

But Thurlow only shrugged. "I don't know anything about pitching. I just got those two weak hitters. It was Trent's throw that saved my fanny. I thought I'd blown the whole game."

"No, no," Trent said. "I don't have a great arm. I just—"

"You just threw the ball *exactly* where it had to be," Robbie said. "You got the job done. Didn't I tell you? That's what this game is all about."

Trent shrugged, but he didn't say anything.

"And you don't brag about anything you do," Thurlow said. "That's what I like." He looked over at Robbie.

"Yeah. I like that, too," Robbie said, and he grinned.

"You don't have to say a thing," Trent said. "You played a *great* game."

By now parents were coming to pick up their kids, and the group was beginning to break up. Robbie yelled out, "Hey, Trent, let's do something tonight."

"Okay. Hey . . . better yet: Let's get the whole team together. Maybe we could go down to the city pool or something—just hang out to-gether."

"Now you're talking," Coach Carlton said. And the word started spreading among the players: Everyone was getting together that night.

TIPS FOR PLAYING LEFT FIELD

1. Don't fall asleep! The action may not come your way all that often, but when it does, you have to be ready. With each pitch, come up on the balls of your feet, ready to move in any direction.
2. Think what you will do on a base hit that you might field. How many outs are there? How many runners? Is the runner on second likely to try to score on a single? If you have thought through the possible plays, you're more likely to make a good decision.
3. Don't take off running until you "judge" the distance of a fly ball. Watch the ball as it comes off the bat, and take an extra split second to decide how well it's hit. Get to the spot where you think it will come down quickly.
4. If you can, catch a fly ball as you step toward the infield. This gives you power in your throw. Even a ball hit over your head, if it's hit high, may allow you time to drop back a little extra distance so you can be moving forward as you catch the ball.
5. Know your own speed. When a ball is hit down the left field line or into left center, what angle can you take to cut it off? Remember, if the ball gets past you, the runner is going to take at least one more base than if you can cut the ball off.
6. Know your center fielder. The two of you must work as a team. How fast is he or she? Is this a

player who can run right and still make a catch?

7. Call for every ball you plan to catch, even if you think it's clearly yours. Yell, "I've got it," and listen for an infielder or the center fielder to respond, "Take it!"

8. If the ball is hit toward center field, the center fielder makes the call. If he or she calls you off, accept the decision and then move into a position to play backup.

9. On a play to short left field, run hard and catch it if you can. Call the infielder off as soon as you are sure you can get to it. It's a much easier catch for you than for infielders, who are running with their backs to the batter.

10. On a ground ball to third base or the shortstop, charge the infield and back up the infielder. If the ball should happen to get through, you'll be there to handle it quickly.

SOME RULES FROM COACH CARLTON

HITTING:

Take some practice swings to relax and loosen up, but when you come set, ready for the pitch, hold your bat still.

BASE RUNNING:

Always listen to your coach. If the coach signals "stop," then do it, even if you're sure you can make it to the next base.

BEING A TEAM PLAYER:

Cheer for your own players, but don't make fun of or yell insults at players on the opposing team. A little "Hey, batta, batta" chatter might be fine, but don't say things that are hurtful. That ruins the game for everyone.

ON DECK:
OLLIE ALLMAN, PITCHER.
DON'T MISS HIS STORY IN SCRAPPERS #4: *NOW WE'RE TALKING.*

Ollie was tense all the next day, and when he took his warm-up pitches before the game, the ball was flying all over the place. He was trying hard to imagine that he was just playing catch with Wilson, but he was sure the team was expecting another disaster, and it was hard to put that out of his mind.

Ollie was also trying hard not to talk to himself. The coach had worked with him at practice. "Think what you want," he had said. "Tell yourself whatever you need to hear. Just do it *inside* your head." It was the same thing Gloria had said, and Ollie knew they were both right.

The first batter was a kid named Waxman. He was fast, but he was no great hitter. The guy would do almost anything to get a walk—and then steal second and third.

So Ollie told himself—inside his head—to get the ball over the plate. Waxman wouldn't swing at the first couple of pitches anyway.

Ollie did everything right on the first pitch.

He didn't throw too hard. He didn't try to hit the corners. He just chucked the ball down the middle. Or at least, that's what he meant to do. But the ball came in hard and low.

So he tried to bring the next one up, and did—way up.

When Ollie got the ball back, he turned with his back to the batter and said, in his mind, "Okay. Stop that. Just throw the ball to Wilson—like you're playing catch. Waxman won't swing."

It was a great idea, but when he turned around, everything changed. He fired the ball hard again. And low again.

And then high again.

Ollie was furious at himself. He had actually walked Waxman on four pitches—a guy who had no bat at all.

Don't worry about Waxman, he thought. But he did worry—a lot. He could see everything falling apart, just the way it had in the last game.

Ollie checked Waxman carefully, wound up, and just as his arm started forward, he saw the guy take off. He tried to hurry the pitch, and he bounced the ball in the dirt. Wilson didn't even make a throw. Waxman had the steal, all the way.

Gloria ran over to the mound. "Ollie, you're forcing your pitches," she said. "You're aiming the ball. Remember what I told you. Just act like you're playing catch, and throw the ball to Wilson. Don't let Waxman worry you."

Ollie nodded. But why couldn't he get his arm to understand what his head knew?

He did get one called strike, but he walked the batter, Wayment, on five pitches.

Sweat started breaking out all over him.

The Pit Bulls were standing up in the dugout, screaming and yelling. "Ollie, Ollie, in free," someone kept saying. "Don't swing, Lumps. He'll walk you."

And up in the crowd, some big guy—someone's dad—kept yelling, "Hey, kid, you couldn't throw a strike right now if your life depended on it."

Ollie was willing to do anything to throw a strike, even if the next batter—"Lumps" Lanman—hit it a mile.

Ollie eased way off, tried to throw a nice, soft pitch that Lumps would at least swing at.

And it almost happened. But the ball had so

little speed on it that it dropped in front of the plate.

Ollie put more mustard on the next one and really popped Wilson's glove—but way outside.

This couldn't be happening again.

The noise was getting worse and worse. People were screaming at Ollie from the bench and the bleachers, and his own players were yelling their support—but with a tone that said, "Please don't do this to us again."

Ollie took a deep breath, tried to think of nothing at all, and just threw the ball to the catcher's mitt. It would have been a perfect pitch had the catcher's mitt been on the batter's ear. But it wasn't, and Lumps almost got a lump.

Instead, he hit the dirt and came up screaming, "Give me something I can hit, Ollie, and I'll knock you off that mound."

That actually sounded like a good idea. An injury would be better than this.

When the pitch sailed high again and the ump said, "Take your base," Ollie was relieved. The bases were loaded, but at least Coach Carlton was walking to the mound. Adam, or maybe Thurlow, would be taking over now.

"Ollie, what's bothering you?" the coach asked.

"I don't know. I can't make the ball do what I want it to."

"Can you go back to talking to yourself, and just keep your voice down? Maybe cover up your mouth with your glove?"

"I don't know. My voice forgets to be quiet sometimes."

"Well . . . try it. I think I got you messed up by telling you not to talk to yourself."

"Okay."

Ollie immediately felt better. As soon as the coach walked away, he whispered, "All right, I'm back." Then he concentrated on Wilson's glove, and he told himself—with his glove over his mouth—"Just see the pitch you want to throw."

This batter was a lefty, a boy named Clark Krieger, and he was leaning in toward the plate. Ollie visualized a pitch on the inside edge—a good, hard fastball.

Ollie took his stretch and checked the runners. And now the picture was in his mind.

Ollie's release felt good. The ball whizzed

close to the batter—a little more inside than Ollie had wanted.

Krieger ducked away. As he did, his bat accidentally swung toward the plate. The ball glanced off the bat and rolled onto the grass.

Wilson charged out, grabbed the ball, and then hustled back to step on the plate. Even Waxman, fast as he was, couldn't get there ahead of him.

One away. And Ollie felt a whole lot better.

Now a guy named Scott Johnson was stepping up to the plate. "Throw *me* that pitch," he called to Ollie. He licked his lips.

Johnson took a couple of slick practice strokes. "He's going to look so stupid when he strikes out," Ollie said, with the glove over his face. "I see the ball at his knees, and hard."

Ollie tossed a perfect pitch—the one he had described to himself. Johnson took a hard swing and missed.

The Pit Bulls seemed surprised that Ollie could find his control. They weren't yelling so much now. But Ollie's own teammates were going crazy. "Now you've got it going," Gloria yelled, and Ollie liked her confidence.

"Go with your curve," Ollie whispered, and Wilson was thinking the same thing. Ollie nodded to the signal, and then he snapped off a curve that broke over the heart of the plate—just as Johnson was backing away.

"*Steeeeriiiiiike!*"

"Now your hard stuff. Bust him down the middle." The voice was clear and so was the picture. Ollie threw a good fastball over the plate. Johnson took a huge cut at it . . . and missed.

"Strike *three*. You're out!" the ump barked.

Johnson tossed his bat away. He wasn't talking now, wasn't even looking at Ollie.

"This is getting to be fun," Ollie told himself. "This next guy doesn't look like a hitter. Throw him some good fastballs, and this inning will be over."